"For Ashley, Connor Baird, Leah, Nicos, Anna, Noah, and all the little true bearers of the Hotty Toddy Spirit."

~Papa Baird

Hotty & Toddy Spirit!

PRT1210A

Printed in the United States.

ISBN-13: 978-1-936319-33-6
ISBN-10: 1-936319-33-0

www.hottytoddyspirit.com

Hotty & Toddy™ Spirit!

T. Baird Morris

Illustrated by

Nate Voss

When Hotty and Toddy were young,

they dreamed of becoming part of the Ole Miss sports teams.

As children they would go to the

Ole Miss sporting events with their parents.

One summer, young Hotty attended cheerleading camp at the University of Mississippi. She saw the many beautiful buildings and landscapes of the campus of Ole Miss.

One summer, young Toddy attended sports camp at the University of Mississippi. He saw many beautiful buildings and landscapes of the campus of Ole Miss.

They were greeted by the friendly students

of Ole Miss attending summer school.

At the cheerleading camp, Hotty met many new friends and learned a few cheers, but most importantly, was introduced to the spirit of Ole Miss.

At the sports camp, Toddy met many new friends and learned to play sports, but most importantly, was introduced to the spirit of Ole Miss.

When Hotty grew older, she fulfilled her dream of becoming an Ole Miss cheerleader, leading students and fans in spirited cheers during a special Welcome Party on the Oxford Square.

When Toddy grew older, he fulfilled his dream of becoming an Ole Miss sports player, leading students and fans in spirited cheers during a special Welcome Party on the Oxford Square.

Now during the summer breaks, Hotty is proud to be an instructor at the cheerleading camps held in The Grove of the University.

Now during the summer breaks, Toddy is proud to be an instructor at the sports camps held on the campus of the University.

A marvelous thing happens for the young cheerleaders

and sports players
attending the camps.

Yes! Each and all saw a part of themselves in the spirits of Hotty and Toddy, and a lot of the Hotty Toddy Spirit in themselves.

HOTTY! TODDY!

Go, Ole Miss!

HOTTY!

TODDY!

GO, REBELS!

GO, OLE MISS!

About the Author

The author and his spouse were born and raised in Oxford, his father being a professor at Ole Miss, and both being graduates from Ole Miss. All of this started in the 1950's, a marvelous time for absorbing the Hotty and Toddy spirit of the Ole Miss campus during its times of tradition and changes. It is the hope that younger children will start their own acquisition of the Hotty Toddy Spirit with this book, if not already benefitted by the spirit. "Papa Baird", the author when around his grandchildren, is now a gnome sunning on the beaches of the Mississippi Gulf Coast, from where he promotes The Hotty Toddy Spirit to all.

"Hotty & Toddy Spirit" is a
HOTTY CHEERLEADER AND TODDY CHEERLEADER
action figure story presentation.

For information about products,
please visit us online at www.HottyToddySpirit.com
or email Hotty@HottyToddySpirit.com
or Toddy@ HottyToddySpirit.com for a catalogue.